AF417425

UNFORGETTABLE

UNFORGETTABLE

DAPHINIE CRAMSIE

Daphinie Cramsie

CHARACTER IDENTITY

NB/NB - Asexual Relationship

CONTENT WARNINGS

Kidnapping, Violence, Blood, Panic Attacks/Disorders,
Death, Injury

To those with longing:
may it always guide you forward
and remind you when to leap.

Unforgettable

Once upon this time, you filtered through dozens of dossiers before selecting them. They had all been qualified, overqualified in fact, but something about this one guard stood out to you. Perhaps it's the way their name sounded in your head, or the easy-going tone in their language when describing their past deeds. Whatever it was, the way their deeds were impressive but still humbly dictated made it feel like they could manage the subtle and serious nature of your mission, even if they are from the Above.

You were due to breach the water soon. Although the water was warm, it didn't keep a chill from running along your spine as it slowly became apparent that your very existence above would put you in danger. Tales of Stenosians being picked apart for spell reagents or to be a headlining curiosity on a stage were parables in your people's folklore. It was no time to lose your nerve. Your people need you to make the trek across the goddess-forsaken land to sign a peace treaty with the Above nations. Things were becoming too risky, too close to home.

Sthenos was supposed to be hidden from the Above. But in the last few years, there had been close call after close call. A pearl diver here, a fishing boat blown off course there, and then soon after, a glass diving bell. There had been negotiations already with the nearest coastal peoples about keeping a tight lip about your nation. However, people can only resist for so long before curiosity consumes them.

Your trusted council pulled you, a scholar, from your studies to reveal that the Above's capital city Arkus was the home of the Above's overall governance system. They had a decades-long peace treaty that barred anyone from revealing discovery. However, the individual nations under that governance bucked and pushed against the boundaries of its rule and guidance quite often.

Now was one of those times and agreements have grown lax. It was time for the treaty to be re-signed. The Under Elders said you were the most trusted of their people, their humble scholar, and they instilled confidence within you in abundance. With a few tidal cycles of travel training, you could keep your people safe. You could be the one that kept your world as it is and has always been.

You felt the burning in your chest. The burning of pride and the pang of fear. You've read so much. So much of life above the surface. It was dry, chaotic, and filled with sadness and strife. It was far from the gentle ebb and flow of tranquility your people lived in.

But there was an ache in your heart. Surely the ache was the craving for adventure, of seeking the unknown. The world would be topsy-turvy to you, but the excitement of what you knew and had yet to know was a craving. To satiate it would mean pulling out of the comforts of your society and its security. It would mean bracing the tides of adventure with the goal of keeping those comforts for others at all costs. To bring the promise of security back to your people would be an honor, a right bestowed to no one else in history. And you knew history. It was your area of expertise, and no one was more knowledgeable than you. It's as if fate had built you for its own.

The waves lapped at you when you breached, and the air was warm. It was a surreal experience to feel the sea like this. The water slid from your skin as you rose, and the weightlessness of the atmosphere was something you prepared for but the way your skin shuddered at the breeze caught you off guard. Your gills spasmed with panic.

As you trudged through the shallow waters, you placed a palm against your belly, finding comfort in the blessed pearl you swallowed that allowed your gills to take in the atmosphere above. On an empty stomach like yours, you could feel the pearl. It was still fresh and large, and the pressing against your abdomen gave you reassurance. Your gills adjusted with this mental coaxing, and you took deep breaths of the air. It would give you thirteen of their moons before you'd need to swallow another one. Just enough time to make it to Arkus and back, the Elders told you.

Your gaze fell past the dark, heavily pebbled shore-line to the beach, and spotted what your history books described as a human upon the large rocks by the shore. Their hair shone a deep brown in the sun, and even from here the scar described in their dossier was present running from their right temple down to their jawline. Human sight might not be as far-seeing as yours, for they didn't even look at you yet, and you took this chance to size up what seemed to be your hired guard, your Keeper.

They seemed to sit upon a bolder with such ease that it cooled your nerves. There was no tense body language conducive to attack. You took a deep breath and steadied yourself by feeling the smoothness of the medallion around your neck. Running your thumb in circles around the pressed metal helped you time your breathing. The heaviness, even more so Above, in your hand kept your mind in the now—kept your inner presence from drifting away from you. Your rucksack that still drained sea water as you waded out of your motherland gave wet squelches as gravity pulled the water from every inch and sloshed around as it emptied.

They didn't notice you yet. They seemed content to scribble notes in a book. Perhaps they'd let you look upon one, feel one in your hand for the very first time. How you longed to feel what was always described as dry, yet smooth. Something you thought generally unlikely due to the Above making everything rough, from rocks to hearts. The tragic dance that water was essential and the Above's life fought tooth and nail against the Sun's one purpose to take it from them was not lost on you.

Their armor looked as if it had seen better days. The bronze pauldrons and gauntlets looked like they were at one time as golden as the sun, and their breastplate was pitted. Upon your closer inspection, you noticed it was even cracked with a messy line of welding keeping it together. It fit their form well and you had no doubt that this armor earned its keep long ago. But wouldn't a successful guard-for-hire replace these relics?

Your stomachs dropped; did you select the wrong escort for this journey? Their physical description matched, but the prestige this one had in their accolades seemed a sure fit of professionalism and dedication. The slapped-on black substance that aged the armor must be important. Perhaps it wasn't the mark of a failure or a mark of weakness in the metalwork. You don't make mistakes. No, not like this. You chose correctly.

You cleared your thoughts as you approached; weight upon one sandaled foot shifted in the pebbled-ridden sand as you grounded yourself. You needed to show just enough tenacity so this guard wouldn't think less of you, but not enough to be aggressive and scare a human away.

This one smirked before placing their pencil between the pages and closed their book before tucking it behind that atrocious breastplate. Your attention went to their eyes, looking past lush lashes to find their eyes a golden brown.

They looked you up and down before their gaze settled on your sandals. Nodding to themself, they took their pack out from behind them and reached out to deposit a set of closed-toe boots on the ground.

"Hello there. You should put these on. That way the tops of your feet don't get sunburned." Their voice was pitched slightly higher than yours, and the way their tone spoke with friendly warmth surprised you. You expected something gruff and curt like a hardened warrior, and much less like a concerned friend. You weren't sure if this was for all humans or just this one.

You knew that your skin would turn three shades of purple from its normal cobalt if you were embarrassed or flustered, which meant you had to keep your wits about you and make sure to keep others in the dark about any intense emotions. With that echoing in your mind, you took a deep breath to process any possible signs of embarrassment. There was no reason to be embarrassed about your footwear. It was something standard even underwater, but you admittedly did not put much thought into anything other than bringing your favorite pair.

You nodded quickly and sat down to switch shoes. You had to trust your guard and show them that you would listen when it came to their experience and specialty.

Showing them this compliance would likely persuade them if matters needed to be taken into your hands at some point. As you slipped them on, you noticed your feet felt wonderful; you could not have made a better fit. Your head tilted as you pondered the chance the guard had guessed your size. Perhaps the Under Elders sent their own dossier to the guard. Yes, that must be it. It would be most logical.

Wanting to make it seem that this was just another day for you and eager to get business out of the way, you poured out a slew of gems and coins from your conch-shaped bag onto your outstretched webbed hand.

The guard shook their head and dismissed your offering with a shrug of their shoulder. "I can't accept that until I've returned you to the sea." They spoke matter-of-factly and ended with a wide grin to drive home that this was standard operation tactics for them.

You were one to correct people, and this was something in the history books of dealings with humans. According to every text, they routinely liked at least half payment upfront. But you decided it was best not to correct them or ask for more details. At least for now. You had to establish that you were professional. That you were indeed a trusted Ambassador.

Once you settled, the guard scooted off the boulder and stood at full height. You weren't expecting it; you were about an inch taller, but their presence felt larger. The confidence with which they held their body and the way they were still so graceful while under plates of armor made you feel secure. The strongest ocean current couldn't drag you away from the gravitational pull of their presence.

"The weather is looking good today; we should be able to make it to camp with some time to spare." They nodded their head to note the clear sky before looking back at you. The crease in the corner of their mouth when they smiled it caused one of your hearts to skip and you cleared your throat to distract yourself from fawning.

"Perfect, lead the way, Keeper…" You knew how to spell their name, but to pronounce it correctly was a different story.

"Aoife. Ee-fuh." They said it slower the second time so you could catch the syllables.

"Keeper Aoife." Your voice mimicked theirs perfectly in pronunciation. You loved languages, and mimicking words was a specialty of yours. You puffed your chest and caught yourself smirking back at them.

They still had the crinkled grin on their face, but the guard's eyes softened when you spoke their name. They hesitated, as if lost in what you said, so you backpedaled, thinking they were waiting for your name. Of course, your name was likely left out of the hiring process for security's sake.

"Scholar Tierin."

Placing your webbed hand to your chest, you bowed, finding the movement happening a little faster than underwater, which caused you to pitch forward.

The keeper stepped quickly and caught you before your face hit the shore. They gently righted you. Trying to collect your composure, you dusted yourself off and avoided their gaze, "Or Tierin, if you're so inclined."

Acting as if nothing out of the ordinary just happened, the Keeper nodded. "Tierin."

You stopped smoothing your clothes into place and looked straight into their eyes. The way they spoke your name with such reverence, with such warmth, caught you unexpectedly. Your cheeks must have flushed, and that's when you first realized the sea wasn't here to calm the tinge across your face. You'd have to continue on with your face giving away everything.

Feeling caught between embarrassment and nervousness, you pulled the canvas hood over your head. Needing to change the subject, you inspected Keeper Aoife's belongings. A large, leathered pack covered in patches made of various materials and an impressively sized canteen bladder seemed to be everything they were to carry. You watched them gear up and mused that equipping a pack and sling of a bladder was like a puzzle when navigating the straps between the various armor pieces.

You found yourself gazing at them again and they seemed unbothered by this. Perhaps they expected a Sthenosian to be curious, but either way, you felt it was improper to linger so you craned your head over them. Your shoulders slumped.

"I admit, I expected a horse when I've read so much about human fondness for them."

"Ah, yes, I'll grab one for us on the return trip. I'd like to make sure we have individual mobility should anything arise."

You narrowed your eyes as the idea that something could go wrong snuck its way into your thoughts. "What are you expecting to arise?"

The guard gestured in front of them as if to push away the worry, "There's always bound to be something, which is why I prepare for everything." They smirked and you could swear their eyes sparkled.

Your hands fingered the strap of your own pack in worry. "And won't that take longer to get to the capitol?"

"Oh, most certainly. Do not fret. I swear I will deliver you to your duty in Arkus in plenty of time. On my honor, I will never get between you and your service." Their smile dropped for just a fraction of a moment. Perhaps this was their professionalism coming through.

They turned before you could ask just how much time they expected. The pearl in your belly must have heard your worry because you swear it ached just then.

As you waited for your guard to collect their things, you noticed a yellow sash wrapped and knotted around their waist. It had to be older than their armor. But it showed care was taken for every fiber. It had been mended multiple times with various levels of skill, and there were embroidered designs in different colors patchworked around it. Even small tokens were sewn to it like a coin of unrecognizable origin, a small piece of iridescent shell, and so forth. A personal talisman, you figured, and made a note to look for something similar on other humans.

You expected the Keeper to stay along the road, but they led you across the field to the edge of the woods before you decided to question it. You had plenty of time to do so, but the transition from sand and pebbles to hard clay, and finally dirt and grass really tested your balance. It took much of your undivided attention to avoid the random divots in the ground and you were surprised how quickly the colors of the sea in their blues and greys grew into greens, ochres, and brilliant speckles of red from the native flora.

The trees were thinly placed here, and their size

was smaller than you expected. You kept the guard in your peripherals, and took the chance to breathe even deeper. It was fascinating how you could still smell the sea from here.

"Is there something down the road that we are avoiding?" You weren't sure you were going to ask when you noticed a road on the other side of that treacherous field.

"No, not at all. There's a small path this way that I know by heart. The canopies will give us some respite from the sun." They spoke over their shoulder and the hitch of their voice told of their excitement at traveling this path.

However, the sun did worry you. You read so much about its different effects from Above and Below. You were prepared to dry out and your guard had submitted a care plan before the arrangement was made official. Trusting a human with your care was hard to do when your whole pilgrimage was to sign a treaty to keep them away.

You had to fight your instincts to not trust another, and having that battle within yourself worried you. Would there be other things you'd have to leave completely in the Keeper's hands? Even below, no one took care of you. You would often get scolded by the Elders for not making room for yourself and your care. How could they ask you not to sacrifice self-care when they turned around and sent you on a dangerous mission where you could very easily meet your maker all too soon?

There was indeed a path, not just along the ground but also through the trees. The Keeper must have trimmed the foliage as they came to the sea this way, for not even one branch was long enough to brush against you. Perhaps you judged the guard's nonchalance a little too seriously, for it was clear that they cleared this area just for you; this detail in preparation was impressive.

As you ventured along the path, the forest seemed to burst with such saturated color and beauty that you kept your mouth open in wonder. Sure, the reefs and stonework Under are beautiful in their own right, but you never imagined that there were so many different shades of green. The way life stretched its way to the sky, no matter flower or tree, was like a hidden poem of fragility and resilience.

You could walk through the lushness of the area all day if they'd let you. And for now, they did. It wasn't until the light through the canopy crowns began to droop that Keeper Aoife paused.

"We've walked some ways; how are you feeling?" They swung their water bladder around and produced a wooden cup.

Taking the offered drink, you greedily gulped it down. They offered a soaked sponge when you had finished. You plucked the swollen sponge from their open hand and the coolness of it eased the dryness immediately. You began to mop it around your neck and exposed areas when you caught the guard looking. Your eyes met for a moment, and they quickly dropped their head and turned to give you privacy.

You chuckled before lowering your hood. You guided your palm above your head to squeeze the sponge to express any remaining water. The liquid cascaded down your slick skin and you felt it diverting around the black globes of your eyes.

"Better." You smiled before standing there with the sponge in your hand, unsure whether to tuck it away with your things or hand it back to the guard in case they also needed it.

The guard, seeing the look on your face as you processed these imaginary scenarios, pursed their lips and blinked slowly, drinking in your expressions.

You could feel the heat going to your cheeks, and you were sure you were flushing violet before the Keeper turned and gave you a reprieve from the attention. You gathered yourself and began to follow the guard, who seemed to have a new-found spring to their step.

"Will we be coming up to town yet?" You hadn't seen one before and could only go off illustrations left in the old stone tomes.

The guard turned around and walked backward on

the trail. They slowed their steps for precaution's sake, and you found yourself closing the distance between you.

"We are sleeping... in a tent, perhaps?" You found your voice hitching up as you glanced over the guard's shoulder to their pack, hoping to see some sort of tent strapped there. Perhaps tents folded down small and that's why you didn't notice it earlier.

"No, just under the sky and tree canopies. Do not fret, I have your bedroll."

You did fret, and you stopped walking to show your uneasiness at the proposed idea of sleeping out in the open. You weren't sure if this was going to work out; surely there would be forest creatures that would come across your camp. You sighed and practiced breathing slowly and steadily, stroking the medallion yet again while nodding your head. It would be all right; the guard would surely change the plans if the topside's weather turned like how you read in those same scrolls about humans.

"I like your necklace."

You thought you misheard them for a moment. Your attention to your breathing was pulled to the guard, who stood with a cocked head. "Oh, thank you." They must have noticed you fiddling with the medallion, which meant they must have picked up on your anxious behavior. "It helps me regulate; something about the smoothness, I guess. I've had it since..." You trailed off there, truly unable to remember just how you had gotten it or when.

The guard clicked their tongue and smiled as if satisfied before turning back to the trail. You followed them. It went on for only a few more hours. Your feet were so sore from being unused to holding all your weight like this, but being able to observe firsthand all the forest had to offer was worth being uncomfortable. You found the dimming light fascinating, as with it came the changing of the guard of forest creatures and plant life. Blossoms curled their petals while birds tucked in their young. Mice braved the surface and they chased each other along the trail and the bases of trees. Your home runs on a tide schedule and much less on a solar one, so to see this change was its own reward.

The sun was still peeking just under the canopy line when the trail slowly opened to a clearing. The guard dropped their pack off and began to push aside small debris. There were larger trees on the outskirts of the area which helped block any heavy breeze. The nearby brush was so thick and voluminous that when seated on the ground, you couldn't see through it. That itself made you more comfortable, as if you weren't quite sitting out in the open.

The guard busied themself pulling out various things from their pack, and you watched intently. They noticed you staring but seemed unbothered by it, to the extent of rolling out your bedroll with a flourish. They had you hold the flintstone, and the glassy texture made you wonder what it tasted like, but as you were lifting the stone to your mouth the guard called over their shoulder. "It's not going to taste great…" They wandered only a few steps away to gather a bundle of firewood that must have been stashed nearby.

You pressed the stone into your palm and moved your attention elsewhere, attempting to act like you were not just about to lick that stone. You stretched out your legs to give your feet a rest when you noticed it was about time. For fire. You've read about it so many times, but here, its summoning was going to happen before your very eyes.

The guard took the stone back from you and struck it several times. Your attention couldn't be pulled away and you found yourself losing time as you stared into the dancing light. The fire itself was small; you did not need the heat, and getting too close would dry your skin, so you scooted your bedroll as close as you comfortably could. Your night vision was great, but the guard didn't see as well as you naturally could, and they seemed to want the light to cook dinner. The small camping pan was cramped with various nuts, greens, and what appeared to be fleshy berries. Once they finished their process, the guard removed them from the heat and put out the flame.

You let a sigh escape you to express your disappointment with the fire's dispersal. "You don't still need that?" you asked, worried about their comfort.

"No, I'm warm enough. It could still be spotted by

pirate patrols along the shore or by bandits along the road. Besides, I wouldn't want to ruin your view." The guard raised their eyebrows and smirked at you.

Not sure if they were looking for a compliment, you let your mouth fall open as you fished for one before the Keeper raised a finger and pointed up.

You followed their urging and looked upon the most brilliant scattering of lights you had ever seen. The crowns of the trees parted just to give you the view of one of the moons and the orbs of light they call stars. It reminded you of the bioluminescence of the deep sea ichthyofauna of your home, which only steeped the display in wonder. Your scholarly soul was pulled to go to them and to explore their mystery.

"They sure are breathtaking." You found yourself marveling at the sight.

"They sure are," the guard responded wistfully without notably looking up.

"We only heard stories of them, but most of our stone scrolls are recounts from fellow Sthenosians. We don't have a lot of Topside tales," you said.

"Would you like to hear one?" The guard poked the still-cooling embers hiding in the fire's ashes.

"Oh, if it wouldn't trouble you too much!" You beamed as you leaned forward, finally taking your gaze off the stars.

"No trouble at all; it's my favorite story."

"And where does it start?" You settled down with your tea and bowl of sauteed greens.

"Where all the best ones do. With a 'hello' or a 'Once upon this time'."

You were certain you fell asleep when the story got to the part with a forked road, which meant the dutiful pair had already realized fate led the way and they made it through the pirate raid... or at least that's where you think the story ended.

When you woke, the guard had already packed and stored all your things save for a bowl of water and another sponge. You let your hand drift in the bowl before submerging the sponge. Expressing the water from it as you refreshed your skin was a simple pleasure that you were thankful the guard understood the importance of. As you moistened your skin, the guard rolled your bed and began to remove any signs that you both occupied this area of the forest.

The pit of your belly grumbled, but it wasn't from

hunger. You fell asleep during the story, which was rude, and your storyteller probably felt insulted.

"I'm sorry, I fell asleep during your story." Your voice was low, and you almost stuttered towards the end of it.

The guard laughed. "Never a need to apologize. It's a long story and I enjoyed being able to tell it. Even if it was just a small bit."

"So, did the pirate cannoneer get exiled or did he realize that he couldn't shake their faith in each other?"

The Keeper threaded their arms through the straps of their rucksack, and they teased you with half-lidded eyes. "Oh well, you'll have to find out tonight."

Succumbing to this as your punishment, you continued to follow the guard out of the clearing and along the path. It was only an hour or so before the forest parted, and the path met a heavily traveled road. The clouds were low and grey, but that didn't bother you. It kept the direct sun at bay and the added moisture in the air was a nice change. It mattered even less when that road led to your very first town.

The guard seemed unimpressed, but by the frequent looks in your direction, you surmised that they were entertained by you taking in the sight of it. Your own cities were generally built in a spiral pattern, but the dwellings inside this town were organized by straight lines. It was all so orderly, and it cemented that these buildings were creations, not at all naturally made. The town was everything you hoped it would be.

The bottom halves of most of the homes were made of stone --- hard and sturdy stone at that. Signs of scorch marks, chips, and variations of the type of stone showed proof of life after struggle. Keeper Aoife informed you when you pointed out the scorches that the village has been rebuilt every few generations; it survived several attempts at being taken over while failing at times as well. But the town is a constant, they informed you; it always comes back anew. They smiled warmly to themself, and you noticed them lost in thought.

You pulled your hood up and flexed your fungal leather gloves to keep you from being spotted, but it might be too much, as the blending of peoples here is magical. Colors burst around you in the form of gorgeous fabrics and paints. Layers of feathers that coated various Aerivians were dizzying as their waltz-like movements were so casual and yet also so beautiful. Occasionally a Bugbear would stroll by, and the thundering of their feet upon the cobbled streets caused the wind chime decorations hanging around homes and market stalls to clink and ring. Humans, like your guard, dipped and wove between them all.

As you weaved through the market, you spied some of the odds and ends on artisan tables that resembled the trinkets sewn onto and into the guard's yellow sash. They must come here often.

You paused at one of the booths, marveling at a pearlescent ring. The shopkeeper offered for you to try it on, and you hesitated. It was important for no one to see you were Sthenosian, and you looked ahead and noticed the guard-sized hole in the crowd. Your stomachs rose in your throat, and you found yourself unable to breathe.

"Hmm, can we see it half a size larger?" The guard's voice came from behind you and over your shoulder. You caught yourself on the verge of hyperventilating, but the guard moved closer and the lack of space between the two of you brought you back. From up against their chest, you felt the security firsthand that they emanated around you. You let your shoulders relax and they fell back to their slack position. The pressure released from your ribs, and for just a moment, you wondered how cool the metal of the guard's armor would be should you rest your face upon it.

The shopkeeper nodded and held up the larger size. Keeper leaned forward, brushing up against the side of your arm, and you startled at the closeness that you manifested.

The guard leaned around you to deposit some coins in the shopkeeper's palm while also wrapping an arm around your waist to keep you from stumbling as bodies in the market packed in. When they straightened back up, they dropped the arm from you and they guided you off to the side of the market. The guard held out the correct-sized pearlescent ring and you brought it to your chest as you caressed the smoothness of it. You couldn't process the idea of just getting a gift from the guard, that it meant more than just a courtesy to you, that was a level of affection to you and your people because the recent moments of not being able to find your guard left you haunted.

"I thought you had gone ahead..." You cast your eyes to the ground, not wanting to let the ache in your voice be accented with an embarrassed face.

"Mmm, fret not, there is no place ahead for me without you."

You raised your head and widened your eyes, taking in the gentle yet intense look on the guard's face as they reassured you. They scooted in closer to avoid an eager customer of the stall behind both of you and you found your hand resting on their chest plate.

"We will rest indoors tonight; there's a tavern here that has just the thing I think you need." The guard looked upon you; you both stayed like that for a moment, and you wished it were longer. As the moments ticked by, you felt something blossoming within you. You were unsure of the feeling exactly, but you liked the mix of queasiness and warmth as it made your hearts race. You'd never felt something like this before, but was clear to you in that moment that it wasn't random but is in fact tied directly with the guard. How quickly you'd allow yourself to get drunk off of it.

There are a few more stops at various booths as the guard filled up on supplies. They mentioned that after this town, the stretch before the next would be long, but with their carefree tone, it became as if the least of your worries. And it was.

The tavern room was up three flights of stairs and was now officially the highest you'd ever been. Looking out on the town made you nervous, so the guard closed the shutters for now. A moment later, a large man knocked at the door with four buckets hanging from the yoke on his shoulders. He nodded respectfully to you both and then began to pour the contents into the large metal drum the guard called a tub.

After several trips, the Keeper paid the man with a few coins and locked the door behind him. The guard effortlessly brought a divider from the corner of the room to the tub and set a chair on the other side facing the door. The labor to provide the tub and water couldn't have been cheap or something you could overlook. To bring the sea to you was yet another gift the guard bestowed upon you. The thought of you being in the guard's thoughts enough to arrange such a thing caught you off guard. Was this evidence that they thought about you as often as you caught yourself thinking about them? Was it insane to think of someone and wonder if you were in their thoughts just as often?

To distract yourself, you went over to the water and sailed your hand through. It was refreshing and you didn't need to be told what it was for. You began to undress, and the guard quickly stepped to the other side of the divider. You could hear them sitting down as the chair squeaked against the floor from the quick movement.

You started to get in and the guard asked quickly, "Would you like me to get your clothes washed? They would be ready before we leave in the morning."

"What would I wear in the meantime...?"

"I have a spare set that's clean and about your size. The cut won't be the best, but it'll do to sleep in."

You inspected your clothing cluttering the ground and you thought about the long stretch ahead. It might be the last time to get them washed; the fibers could use some care to make them softer, but the lack of not having your personal clothing makes you hesitate.

You pushed the clothing towards the end of the divider with your webbed foot and climbed into the tub. "Yes, that would be lovely." You articulated your words with a cadence and a whispered singing tone saved for close friends, and the shadow of the guard tensed; they noticed the change in your voice but said nothing.

You watch the silhouette moving across the divider

to its end and leaning over to gather your clothing. The rustle of a bag and the door being opened for a moment caused you to sit up in the tub and lean forward to better your hearing. You weren't sure if your guard left with your clothing, but after a beat, you heard them shuffling around the room and the clinking of metal as they removed their armor.

You settled back into the water, content that the guard hadn't left, and slid to submerge yourself completely under. The sound of the prying floorboard and creaking aged wood broke through the damping of the water around you. Curious, you sat up. "What are you doing?"

"I have some things stashed here. I keep some clothes and other trinkets around various places I frequent. More secure than the bank holds." The answer was so matter-of-fact as if everyone did this.

The water was great, but your curiosity was greater. You pondered just what someone would stash around. What would they need to keep hidden in various places, and for what purposes would they need to be retrieved? You fought the urge to ask more as you figured being polite should be more of a priority.

You leaned back against the cool metal, and you saw the guard had cracked the window open. From this angle you couldn't see the height you were from the ground; all you could see was the open night sky warmed by the town's lanterns and the glow of life. The light of the stars fought through the town's luminance, and you found their everlasting presence comforting.

The stool next to the tub had a cloth over it. Curious, you leaned forward and removed the cloth. It was lighter weight than you thought, and it drifted to the edge of the divider before you could catch it. Under it was a slice of cake and a small metal pitcher full of liquid. Your throat clicked to express curiosity and it was loud enough for the guard to hear.

"Lemon cake; I thought you might like it. The pitcher has some oils for your bath, should you like something a little more nourishing." From the scratches and scritches it sounded like the guard was back to writing in their book.

You smelled the pitcher, and you weren't sure what it smelled of but was wonderful. You poured it in and floated in the water before grabbing the cake. It was tart and sweet, and everything you wished you would be eating when you were dreaming of this place from Undertow.

The shirt and pants fit loose, but well. You had stayed a few hours in the tub but found yourself drifting away, so when the guard draped clothing to sleep in over your divider, you felt the push to leave the tub. Just like the guard said, they were perfect for sleeping. It was only when the candlelight was blown out that you noticed there's just one bed. You looked over your shoulder to ask the guard about it, but they were already padding their bedroll down near the side of the bed. The covers of the bed had been turned back for you and they looked so welcoming.

A night in a bed had been on your wish list and it looked incredibly soft. Sliding into the spot, you relished the linen against your skin and the pillow was like a bed of sea moss.

For a moment, you thought of home and everyone waiting for you to finish signing the treaty so all can be set right. Your chest tightened and your neck tensed as it all weighed down on you.

"The cannoneer did let them go."

You caught your breath, confused, and looked down at the guard, who was lying on their bedroll with their eyes closed.

"The cannoneer...?"

"Mmhmm. Just went up and let them go. They say it's because he saw the spark when they looked at each other. It reminded him of his lost love, and how much he wished he could be with him just for one more day. So, he let them go."

You remembered it's the story was cut short before. You'd been waiting for the next part, so when the guard started it up again you did your best to slow your breathing so you could hear every word and not your thundering hearts.

Anything to keep your mind from dwelling on the closeness of you and the guard.

"H-he told them that?" You whispered a curse to yourself for your stutter. Why couldn't you just talk normally?

"Mmm, not both of them that time." The guard didn't seem to notice the stutter or felt it wasn't something to comment on. Your colleagues back home were always quick to comment on it no matter the frequency or how you asked them not to.

"Did they know it about each other?" Your fingers absentmindedly fiddled with the top edge of the sheet.

"Know what?" The guard peeked an eye open.

"About the spark, the sparkle they had for one another?" You were well-read and knew that the spark really meant a blossoming love and longing. Something you couldn't relate to but now...

The guard closed their eye again and grinned smugly. "One of them did, but they didn't tell each other yet."

"Why not? What was stopping them from confessing?" You could guess what, but this pair was different; they had been through so much.

"Well, that would be the dragon."

You shot forward in bed and craned over the edge to look down on the guard. "Excuse me, what!?"

They chuckled and reached their hands under their head while keeping their eyes closed. "The dragon. It was a total surprise. No one even knew there was one in the area, let alone headed straight for the town..."

You laid back down, pulled the covers up, and listened yet again until you slept, keeping your eyes on the open window. Just in case any dragons flew into focus.

Unlike the day before, the story continued. After leaving the town and continuing the hike forward, your guard filled in details and added to the story. Through the fields of wheat that were taller than you, you found out the adventurers chased a runaway carriage that secretly held royalty inside.

When your path diverted and met large river rapids, uneasiness creeped into you. Fast moving water was dangerous, even to sea-bound creatures. The guard took your belongings as well as theirs and crossed a large fallen tree trunk first. They deposited the items on the other side before returning to you. The ease with which they crossed the trunk was reassuring. If they could traverse it to and fro, then surely you would make it safely across.

They took your hands in theirs and gave them a gentle squeeze. You didn't even notice that they had reached out for you, and you had eagerly held them in return until they released your hands to cross back over the river. They stood on the other side with their leg hiked up on the tree as if they were comfortable and completely confident in your ability to cross. You stepped up on the trunk and the guard began the next part of the story.

An ancient fear of death plagued you when you glanced down; the ways your life would end if you fell flashed in your thoughts. The guard clapped their hands loudly to get your attention and they began to shout the story as if this was just another day. You welcomed distraction.

"BUT HOW DID THEY KNOW IT WAS HIM?" Your legs trembling, but you urged them to take a step and then another.

"WELL, ARES' SIGHT WAS NOT TO BE DIS-REGARDED. WHEN THEY FIRST MET THE MAN AT THE DOOR, HE NOTICED BLOOD DRIED UNDER HIS NAILS." The guard smiled wide enough for the corner of it to crinkle again.

"HOW DID THEY KNOW IT WAS BLOOD?" Another few steps.

"THEY DIDN'T, NOT TILL LATER, BUT IT

MADE SENSE AFTER THEY SAW THE BODY." The Keeper held out their hand to you as you came closer.

"AND DESTOS JUST WENT WITH IT?" You kept up with the questions while the guard seemed to enjoy answering them, just so you could not focus on the turbulent rapids beneath your feet.

"Of course, Destos trusts Ares with their life, so trusting in their intuition was easier than breathing." The guard clasped their hand around yours when you reached for them and the other rested back on your waist to guide you down from the large tree trunk safely.

A rather impressive stone crossroad checkpoint, complete with a slew of guardsmen, tightened your chest until the Keeper drew you close. With an arm around your back, they whispered about how the heroes broke into a rather vivacious retired war hero's abode to return a long-ago stolen sword. Papers were stamped and coins were paid, so once you were approved by the guardsmen, the Keeper let their voice return to normal volume.

The town that the heavily patrolled road led to gave you the first indication of the guard taking something more seriously. Their body stiffened and their breathing was tight. Their normal chatter was gone, and they kept close to you, eyes scanning each and every person who came near you. You asked if there would be trouble, and the guard attempted a reassuring smile but didn't answer you. It had only been two days, but you'd memorized every curve of their lips. They couldn't fool you with a forced smile. They told you not to worry, but you did anyway. You realized if something could make them uneasy it was worth you also worrying. Perhaps the guard didn't want to worry you, or perhaps they knew if they spoke the lie, you'd see through it.

Unlike the last tavern, this one didn't have a tub. The guard apologized and stated that they didn't know the current owner. They had won ownership in a duel over spilled mead and heavy accusations of cheating. A lack of a tub for the night would be fine; your skin had plenty of time before it would need to be submerged in water, but when the guard brought in extra water for your sponge, it helped ease the disappointment caught in your tense shoulders.

You were going to invite them to sleep on the bed with you. It was a shame to waste the large size and to leave the guard on the floor when the bed was perfectly fine. You knew the implications that sharing one's sleeping space meant intimacy. It surprised you that you would allow, let alone crave, the closeness of their presence. You pulled back the invitation from your lips as you pondered if the guard would crave the same closeness. Before you could overcome your hesitations, the guard settled on the floor with their head against the bedpost. They kept the window and the door within their sightlines. You drew the blankets up closer to your chin and your breath hitched in your chest, but then your eyes landed on your guard. Your guard. And your breath eased.

The slamming of a door broke through your dreamless state. It was still dark when you shot awake. The guard was up against the door with their hand on the knob. They looked over at you and lifted a finger over their lips. They cracked the door open and peered out before closing it again and silently making their way back over to you. Seeing their reaction to a sound that seemed innocent and standard in a tavern made your breathing quick and you pulled the covers higher over you.

"Please, get dressed and get your pack together," the Keeper said.

"W-what's going on?" You didn't waste time waiting for a response as you slid out from the warm comfort of the bed. You quickly changed and jammed everything you could into your pack, allowing your task to keep your focus.

"I'm not sure, and I don't like it."

There was a loud creak from the hallway and the guard tensed. Their voice dropped to a whisper. "I'm going to check it out. Stay here, stay quiet." They took a few steps back to you. "I'll be right back."

The guard stepped out and headed down the hall.

You heard a loud crash, stumbling, and some voices grunting. The severity of the moment led you into a panic and you craned your neck at the door, desperate to hear any word from your guard.

The door flew open and instead of your guard came a figure in dark blue robes. Its ominous form filled the doorway. It dove towards you, accosting you in such a way that you had trouble escaping their grasp. You did for a moment — your strength was impressive — but they knew the area, and were familiar with the way the world works up here. They caught your foot as you ran down the hall.

You yelled as loud as you could and projected sounds of distress from your gills. As you ran, you yelled for the Keeper. Your screams for them were met with silence. Your guard or any evidence of them was nowhere to be seen.

You fell and held your palms out to take the brunt of it, but you still scraped your face against the wooden floor. The figure in blue hauled you up and pulled you down the hall with renewed strength.

You were pulled and pushed down the stairs, and through the kitchens. Each corner you took, you expected to see the guard coming to you, and each time you were disappointed. Fear slammed into you when you saw the horses and carriage waiting. This was it. The warnings, the tales of the danger you would face, were here and were happening now.

You were shoved into the back of the carriage and two dark blue-robed figures climbed in. The one that took you grabbed the reins and began the drive. Everything was moving slower and slower, but your hearts beat faster and faster. Your vision blurred and each second that you accepted this was happening only called an inky dread into every inch of you, threatening to drown you from the inside. But the dread wasn't for you; it was for your guard. Your future was clear as the waters of your home, but theirs? Theirs was unknown, and that chilled you.

The horses pulled with such velocity that the three of you inside fell against the floor. That's when you noticed the blood seeping from one of the figures' sides. Your guard. They must have fought back and injured one of them. The figure caught you looking and sneered as if it was directly your fault that they were injured during your kidnapping.

Your ride evened out, the horses grew steadier, and you could see the shoulders of the kidnappers drop from tension through the window up by the driver. The carriage lurched suddenly to the right. One of the bandits reached through the small window's opening to tap the driver's back for attention. The response was the driver falling off to the side with a crossbow bolt sticking out from between their shoulder blades.

You didn't understand the language, but the other two shouted at each other. One of them started to climb through the driver's window as the carriage rumbled to a stop. You kept peering at the carriage doors. Who was there — more bandits? Your hearts felt like they would burst with the speed of their beating.

Just then, there was a loud, piercing scream as the figure who climbed only halfway through the window, now stuck with the realization of how small the window was, was pulled savagely outside, leaving smears of blood from a body too large for the hole.

You held your breath as you trembled. The animal-like attack on the figure pushed you to hold your breath, but the carnage bothered you less as it set in that these were the kidnappers. That these people in dark blue robes were also present in cautionary tales of Sthenosian dissections. Perhaps if you were quiet enough, whatever attacked them would pass you by.

It didn't take long for the screaming outside the carriage to stop, but the figure left inside was as quiet as you. They shook in place and a puddle formed at their feet. Although a natural reaction, it still slightly disgusted you. They could cause harm, but when it was turned against them, it was too much. You scooted to the side to avoid the puddle and the bandit let their handful of your tunic slide from their grasp.

The carriage doors were tossed open, and the bandit threw a dagger through the opening only to have it clatter on the cobblestone road. There wasn't anything there.

As if summoned by the moonlight or the cries for help leeching out from your soul, your guard stepped into the light. They held out an open palm to you and managed to smile, but their eyes stayed on the bandit. "Would you like to come with me?"

You nodded quickly and inky dread retreated as you took healthy gulps of air. You scooped your things from their tossed position on the plush bench, and when you looked back to the Keeper you noticed the gauntleted hand not holding yours was held secretively behind their back.

"If you could be so kind as to wait for me on this side of the carriage..." They guided you to the side with a beautiful view of a pond. You didn't find your words yet, but with each new breath, you released tension. The guard was here. It was going to be okay.

Wood creaked and the clinking of shifting metal announced that the guard climbed back into the carriage and close the doors politely behind them. There were more whispers from the bandit in the unknown language, but you didn't hear a word from your guard. You could already identify the sound of just one of their sighs out of a crowd. Now, the sound of metal on meat did not stop until the scrape of metal on wood echoed across the pond.

You were not ignorant of the happenings around you. You were neither young nor inexperienced with combat, so it was easy for you to watch the yellow moth float across the sky. The yellow reminded you of the guard's sash, which caused a smirk to creep across your lips.

The doors closed and your guard came back out. They were wiping off their gauntlets on a dark blue cloth, which they tossed aside when they approached you.

They held their hands out to you and when you held their metal covering, you grimaced. You didn't find comfort in cold steel. You wanted to feel them. You wanted the comfort of their warm hand in yours. The guard seemed to notice your look and hurriedly removed them, letting them drop to the ground carelessly just to hold hands.

You both locked eyes.

"I am so sorry that you experienced that. I want you to know that I will *always* come for you. Even time cannot keep me from you. Should there be a moment you wish to be apart from me, I will respect your wishes. Just say when."

You didn't know you said it until it already escaped your lips. "Never."

That was when you saw the sparkling look in their eyes and knew it was in yours too.

The guard caressed your hands with theirs and

then nodded to the front of the carriage. "We'll go on horse from here."

Moments later, you were on horseback. Your newly acquired horse trotted alongside theirs. It took a slight adjustment for you to get the hang of it. "A natural," the guard told you. It felt like it too. You had ridden deep-sea beasts, so the idea was the same, although the side-to-side movement was now replaced with an up-and-down trot.

When you had reached a spot to rest, the guard set up your tents as you found kindling for the small cooking fire. You worked while humming and you could swear you heard the guard humming along. Which would be impossible; the song you hummed was from the Under.

It wasn't until the fire was lit and the night was upon you both that you noticed the guard kept their side covered with the crook of their arm. You pulled at it gently; the guard gave in to you, and you took in the sight of blood seeping through the fabric. Stupid, you thought to yourself. You didn't need them to hide it from you. They should have said something earlier. You could have helped.

You fought through your disappointment and bit your lip in frustration. "Lay down." You didn't expect the guard to complain, and they didn't. Using the yellow sash as a rest for their head, the guard pulled off their breastplate and most of their armor, and that was when you noticed just how much bulk the armor added. Now it was just the two of you.

You pulled the shirt up and noticed blood coated most of their abdomen in various states of dried and fresh. There was also some very shoddy poultice work. You remembered that on the ride here, the guard seemed to be shoving something under their shirt, but you dismissed it. With flittering fingers, you managed to clear most of it off so you could see.

As if embarrassed, they said, "I couldn't quite get to it to stitch it up…"

"I see that." You rummaged through your pack that the guard had recovered, and found your med kit, lovingly prepared by the healer elders. You spread the work cloth. Stopping a bleed and closing a wound was taught at a young age in the Under. Blood in the water was something to be avoided at all costs.

Unlike the Above, instead of stitching, a glue-like substance was the norm. There were members of your society who spent their time farming and milling the substance into perfection.

You mixed what you could and began to clean the wound with the compound, only stopping to add a branch or two to the fire to keep the guard warm.

Their chest bindings shifted as you worked, and you delicately reached over to adjust them. From the corner of your eye, you caught the guard smirking and then closing their eyes.

"With the tree pod held between their horses, they had no choice but to take the main road. But, that meant Blixington's Company was something they could no longer avoid."

The continuation of the story made you feel minnows in your belly and yet also a sense of calm as the guard told it. You managed to ask, "But, isn't Blixington himself a prolific bounty hunter?"

"Very much so. And there's that one bounty from the coast that's been skyrocketing in reward tokens…"

When you finished dressing the wound and putting back your things, the guard gently stretched upwards to make your honey tea on the fire. You didn't ask, but it was exactly what you wanted. They continued the story, answering your questions and nodding to your insightful comments, and it was that night you wished it wouldn't ever be dawn again.

The next few days were wonderful. You opened up, telling stories about your family and your studies. You both switched off as the guard continued to tell you more about this adventuring pair, and you would get so worried that you'd begin to overheat. So, you both would have to stop and wait under a tree for you to cool back down.

The guard never seemed bothered by these interruptions. It gave you time to ask questions about each flower on the ground and each bird in the sky. One stop, a particularly rowdy sparrow caused you to leap up and point it out to the guard, knocking them over in the process.

You noticed they checked the map less and less the closer to the capital you got. But, if the guard noticed you looking at their frown, your eyes would meet, and their look would soften into the most wonderful smile.

You spotted the capital on the horizon, and it loomed like a giant. Even from a distance, it felt like less of a city and more like a living entity of its own. The capital and all its dwellings were built out of the most brilliant white stone. The city gates were glorious in their highly detailed metalwork and in their several-stories-tall heights. You were unsure how they even managed to open the big doors, but you ended up deciding it must be from magic.

You were enamored with the architecture, the mix of metal and stone, and the glow of magic within the city. Nothing was quite like this under the water. You also, with sadness in your heart, realized that nothing from your world was here either. Your dwellings were made of stone as well but also compressed of ocean sand that formed a delicate-looking glass. Coral and home gardens grew on the walls outside of most dwellings. Techniques from home would surely add to the beauty and mechanical efficiency of the city here, but the entire lack was a little startling, and the growl of homesickness rumbled. This lack was exactly why you were here. There couldn't be anything from home; there couldn't be anyone from Above to stumble across your civilization. It would be unsafe for your people, the Under Elders told you.

There were scrolls of times past of a stranger who happened upon the city, and they quickly attempted to apply claims of ownership to your nation. It took many lives and many years to convince the Capital Elders to help.

One of the guard's legs brushed up against yours as they scooted close to you in the city streets, watching every corner, every cart, and every window. You mimicked their watchfulness. You could be that protector for them too. You wanted to be that. You wanted it so badly.

There were a few stops along the way; a carver caught the Keeper's attention who made a quick purchase of a mother-of-pearl cloak clasp with a beautiful rendering of a sparrow. You only knew it was a sparrow from one of the stops under a tree. You remember the nest the sparrow flew to, and the memory of the recent hatchlings looking over its edge caused a light laugh to slip from your lips. You watched the guard and noticed they didn't put it on, just placed it in their pocket and continued on.

You wondered just who they were saving it for. A large

clasp like that didn't seem to be your guard's style, as they preferred things small enough to attach to their sash. There were more stops, food, and drinks as well, but as you got closer to the center citadel, you lost your appetite.

It was time.

Time to re-sign the treaty between the Citadel Elders and your people.

The guard approached you with a plate of warm pastries. The joy of sweets was spoiled by the looming duty. Your slight frown must have given you away. The guard's casual smirk dropped to match your frown. They knew.

"Perhaps after." You managed a smile, but it was a few odd beats before the guard returned the smirk, and you noticed a practiced mask rise across their face when the sparkle in their eye began to harden. They wrapped the pastries in a wax cloth and placed them in their satchel.

"Are you ready?" There was a pain in their voice, but you appreciated the seriousness in the manner. When you nodded, you felt a heaviness around the both of you.

The citadel was made of the same white stone, and as it rose into the sky, glass panels depicting various figures made up its windows. It was heavily guarded. The sentries here had armor similar to your guard's, but with a quick inspection, you knew your guard's armor was as unique as them. Your guard raised their bare hands as you both approached.

The sentinels of the citadel recognized the hand signals the guard presented to them and you were both ushered inside while they stowed your horses.

With each step, you trudged up floor to floor, and your body grew heavier. Not from the height, but from the weight of duty. The exertion of it all pressed against your chest, and your breathing became difficult. The guard reached over to give your hand a reassuring squeeze, but you threaded your fingers in theirs before they could pull back. Their thumb tapped the beat of the song you hummed on your journey. The corners of your mouth lifted in a smirk.

It was several floors up before a warden in golden armor stopped you both. The elders were beyond, and even your guard, your escort, was not allowed past this point. You parted and you took a few steps forward before turning back around.

Your guard nodded and you smiled. "I'm not sure how long this will take, but you'll be here when I'm done?"

The guard's warmth returned. "Of course; there's nowhere else I'd rather be." You found yourself reaching for their hands and they quickly took them, their thumbs caressing your fingers. The sparkle returned and you could feel yours too.

"Perhaps we can take the long way back? I must hear more of the adventurers." You'd make plans too — plans to not return to the sea. You could stay here. With them. You were greedy for more of the stories that seemed to never end. Adventure after adventure, after adventure, after adventure, after adventure.

"As you wish."

You squeezed their hands once more and let them go, turning back to the golden warden as he led you down the hall. You looked back to find the guard still there. Steadfast. And it looked like they had untied one of the bobbles from their sash, a steel ring with a pearl inlay, and slipped it upon their index finger. That specific finger was reserved to indicate betrothal. You wondered if this custom was the same here Above.

"This way," the warden huffed, and he took you down a hall away from the center. It was a few rooms away before you noticed the lighting getting darker and the decorations less regal. That familiar inky dread rose within. Your own voice screamed in your head that something was wrong. The voice was cut off when you were slammed against the wall, the air in your chest forced out in an audible gasp.

The golden knight had withdrawn a dark steel dagger and held it against your throat.

"Let me go," you gasped.

"Not a chance. One of your kind will fetch me endless riches and it'll only cost me you."

You were so disgusted that heat rose in your face and anger bubbled molten in your heart. "And your honor as a Keeper of Arkus?"

"Hah. Honor is for dreamers and romantics."

Your people needed you, and you were so close. You just had to sign the damned paper. Why couldn't this nonsense happen after? Why would this lone person be the downfall of your homeland? You'd fight back, of course, but a Keeper of Arkus' skill was legendary. You were a scholarly pacifist, not a warrior.

The knight's other hand lifted your chin, and you could feel the muscles under your skin buckle from the pressure, bruises likely forming already with the tension. You slammed your eyes closed, preparing for the moment.

After it didn't come, you peeked your eyes open to find the knight's grasp on your chin growing slack and blood bubbling out of his mouth, dripping down the front of that oh-so-golden armor. The flash of a hand adorned with a steel ring with a pearl inlay pulled the man off you as a gruff tone growled in his ear. "You don't get to touch xem."

The golden one fell when a long blade was completely unsheathed from the length of his back, hilt having breached the security at the bottom rim of his backplate, and there stood your guard. They dropped the sword when you rushed into their arms, shaking from adrenaline and you burrowed your head into their neck.

They didn't say anything, just held you and took deep breaths which helped you match to your own. You weren't sure how long you both stood there.

"How did you know?"

"Destos could always feel when Ares was distraught." The mention of the story warmed your heart, and you pulled back, eyes gazing.

"And you'll be my Destos?"

With a gentle hand, the guard cleared the blood from your cheek. "Always."

Your hand crept up and held the back of their neck. Their breath was warm against your skin, and you could hear their thundering heartbeat this close. You rested your forehead against theirs and with a slight turn, your lips brushed each other's.

It felt like forever and no time at all that you stood there, anchored in each other's embrace. Footsteps thundered close as another golden-armored warden rounded the corner with several robed officials.

"Here they are!"

Your eyelids widened at the declaration and you moved yourself behind the guard. What now? you pondered. What else could possibly happen?

They all rushed forward. As you released the guard you saw *them* in the flesh. The Citadel Elders. The seven of them were often described in your studies, their immortality gifted long ago for their bravery and the never-ending quest to spread knowledge. Their individual accolades were embroidered on their ceremonial robes. A cloaked one behind the group was the only one who did not speak as they all ushered in a wave of apologies and reassurances.

It was a whirlwind, but you were led back to the center of the citadel. The multi-story tower had a library as its core which was guarded by more sentinels. Those guards traded nods to yours.

Your guard stood at the open door, unable to go inside. Their eyes were on you alone, never straying to the crowd of Elders behind you or to the decadent library through the doorway. Their practiced smirk was up and present again, but their eyes held a sadness so deep that it took everything in you not to go console them.

"Don't worry, I'll be right back." It couldn't take too long to sign the treaty that was already drafted and approved by the Under Elders. You were told of course to read it thoroughly, to make sure there were no additions or changes, but you had to memorize the treaty by heart so you could make quick work of performing your duty.

"We can get more of that lemon cake to celebrate after."

The guard smiled, their eyes still betraying the longing in their eyes. "*As you wish.*" The Keeper's slip into your mother tongue was effortless. You hadn't heard of a human being capable of the subtle echoes and trills of the language before.

"Ha, you speak Sthenian so well."

"I have had an amazing teacher."

You made a mental note to have them tell you all about the teacher and how it was that they had learned it at all. How long it must have taken to master...

You stepped away with a nod and entered the library. You had to make it back to your guard. It was clear that it was your turn to take care of them, and you couldn't wait to show them the care that would be the expression of your love.

The treaty was exactly as promised, without any changes or additions needed. Well, until you get to the last page. Confused, you looked up to the six Elders who were posted around the library, waiting for you to finish.

"What's this...?" They must have known exactly what you were referring to as they all looked upon you with great sadness.

"It's a piece that is required for this to truly work, Ambassador." One Elder stepped forward.

"I don't understand when it says 'The world untouched by the Goddesses Three will forget Stenos'... I'm sorry, I just don't get what that means."

Another one of the Elders scooted closer to you and spoke so softly it was like they were worried you were glass and would shatter from a louder tone. "Anyone not touched by all Goddesses Three directly will forget that Stenos exists. Any items that might linger here will be classified, and texts written by the hands of those unblessed will become blank. The safety of Sthenos and those Under will be secure again."

"And what of those Under? We've been touched with immortality; will we be affected?"

"Yes. Those Under were only given a blessing by one of the Goddesses, so those untouched by all three will forget about any encounter with those Above."

"So, I-I'll forget everything, everyone?" Your pulse pounded and your breath quickened. This couldn't be happening. No, not now. Not when you've finally found them.

The Elder standing near the stained-glass window depicting the might of the sea stepped forward. "Yes, you will forget. Our people, the Sthenosians, are blessed, but it's not enough. The memory of those Above must be dissolved." She lowered her hood to reveal herself as a Sthenosian. Her large golden globe eyes matched yours in form but not color. "It's the only way to keep everyone truly safe, and yes, even your adventure here will be forgotten."

Tears pulled at your eyes. There was a fable that Sthenosians couldn't produce tears, but they do; the water just whisks the sadness away. But here above, you are left to wallow in it.

It meant you would forget your guard. Your guard would forget you. Everything between you would cease to exist. Your body's weight pressed into the plush seat, and it felt like you were looking at yourself from outside. Could you just float away, just now? The tears flowed down your cheeks and landed in your palms, which you dropped heavily into your lap. There were so many that they collected into tiny pools, and you could see yourself reflected in them.

The Elders were patient and did not leave your side.

"If you do not sign, your people will continue to be discovered, documented, and there will likely be a repeat of the time of Raknos."

"But — if the Elders don't forget, can't you figure out another way!?" You shuddered between your loud sobs.

"Our oath and our agreement in exchange for the blessings of the Goddesses Three was that we could not interfere. We can only assist in what Her peoples agree upon."

Forget this love, forget the only one that made you feel infused with life, or doom your people.

"Will you take care of them?" you sniffled. "Will you make sure they always have an ear for their stories? Will you make sure they always have a fire lit to keep them warm? Sometimes they forget to feed it, so you'll have to make sure to add more anyway. Will you make sure they know someone loved them?" Your hand reached for the quill and the Elders nodded slowly, all seeming to know exactly to whom you were referring.

"We will."

* * *

It was hours before the door opened and I was able to come in. Even though it had been a long time, it was still so strange to be on this side of the door. I left the Citadel Elders long ago, when I could no longer trust others to accompany you on your journey.

The Citadel Elders prepared your bags after you fell into the forgetting. The slumber would last days. For you, the Ambassador, the spell worked immediately. You would be asleep until I placed you back into your home waters, where your people, blessed by the most hopeful of the Goddess Three, would be waiting for you. The rest of the world would forget over the span of a few days. The area around the citadel and around the shore nearest your home would forget first and then radiate out until the entire globe was swallowed in the ritual spell.

"Would you like a carriage this time?"

I shook my head. They offered every time, and every time I denied them. I would carry you. Every step, every second that I could. I would carry you safely, just as Destos carried Ares.

I changed our names in the story; it was less alarming when I could slip into part of the tale. But each time you'd be more and more eager to hear our story.

You were peaceful when you slept, although your face was drenched from your tears. I reached over to wipe off the trail of them with my fingers, careful to smooth your skin with each pass and not press. Too much pressure caused you to break out and you'd fret so much when your skin would break out.

My tears would come too. I waited to process my grief

over your absence after I returned to you safely. My duty to you hasn't yet ended.

I lifted you from the lounge and carried you through the threshold. I mounted the horse waiting for me. Our way back to the shore was efficient. I didn't stretch it out like I did on the trip to the citadel each time.

I couldn't risk the blessed pearl lasting less than the allotted time and have you awaken, your gills gasping for air only to find yourself being carried away on land by a stranger. It was better for you to reach the shore and awaken in your own bed, at home where your people would be safe.

Safe for a time, until humans eventually got too curious and found your people again. Then it would repeat again and again. Like it has been. Your people had an average of being discovered every twenty years or so.

And each time, I'll be there. I'll be there for you when you rise from the sea. I spend my time between your visits in an old lookout near the coast. The one we bought with the spoils of that cavern rescue up north. I sit at the bay window looking out into the sea and wait. I'll be there when you rise up on our favorite boulder that we were married on a couple of times before. I'll take you to the Citadel to fulfill your duty each time. There will be times like before when we would get swooped up into a local disagreement or run away for a spell and become pirates or, as you noted at the time, privateers, upon the sea but we always come back. Each time you decide to protect your people even if it means forgetting me, forgetting us, and I fall in love with you more.

I pinned the cloak brooch to your clothes. Sometimes the Under Elders let you keep the items I leave for you, like the medallion; other times I'm sure they stole them away. And each time, I sew something of us onto the shawl you made for me on our first voyage, just the two of us. Every piece was a fragment of yet another time we fell in love.

Although this will be the 1,534th time I've placed your sleeping body back in the water, I'll be here for another and another.

I will always be here, and I will always fall in love with you and fall in love with loving you. And maybe, just maybe there will be a time that Ares and Destos can finally be Tierin and Aoife, and maybe there will be a time no one has to forget our greatest love story ever told.

Until then, my love, I'll remember enough for the both of us.

ACKNOWLEDGEMENT

Thank you to my mother for always instilling that magical worlds whether real or not are always just as meaningful as this one. My love for books and adventure started with silly voices, bedtime stories, and you insisting the last page of the story doesn't mean it's the end.

To Becca Johnson who was here from the beginning when I had less than a solid idea and more of a rambling. I couldn't ask for a better Developmental Editor and Book Coach than you. Without you, this story would simply not exist.

Always to my husband. Your love for stories no matter the format and the constant support kept me going when all I wanted to do was give up.

To Azalea Crowly and R.N. Barbosa who put together Love, Ace, and Monsters the Ace Anthology where this was originally published. They took a chance for someone with no stories to show of their own and gave me a home and a way to reach others just like us.

Thank you to Elizabeth Thurmand who also worked on copyediting and proofreading. And to my friends and family who read earlier copies and gave such uplifting support.

To readers who this is all for. You are enough and always have been. Proclaim from the furthest stars and from the deepest seas that you, your opinions, and your worth are undefinable.

ABOUT THE AUTHOR

Daphinie Cramsie

Rumor is Daphinie (she/her/they/them) is really just three kobolds in a trench coat. They live in the SW United States with two spawnlings and a husband that is also likely to be yet another three kobolds in a slightly longer trench coat. Somehow they all live with a cat, and three dogs.

Find them online at
www.daphiniecramsie.com

9 798869 142726